# Mr. Putter & Tabby
# Run the Race

CYNTHIA RYLANT

# Mr. Putter & Tabby
# Run the Race

Illustrated by

ARTHUR HOWARD

Harcourt, Inc.

Orlando   Austin   New York   San Diego   London

HALF HOLLOW HILLS
COMMUNITY LIBRARY

*For Eamon Johnston, who runs a good race*
*—C. R.*

Text copyright © 2008 by Cynthia Rylant
Illustrations copyright © 2008 by Arthur Howard

All rights reserved.
No part of this publication may be reproduced or transmitted
in any form or by any means, electronic or mechanical, including
photocopy, recording, or any information storage and retrieval system,
without permission in writing from the publisher.

Requests for permission to make copies of any part of the work
should be submitted online at www.harcourt.com/contact or mailed
to the following address: Permissions Department, Harcourt, Inc.,
6277 Sea Harbor Drive, Orlando, Florida 32887-6777.

www.HarcourtBooks.com

Library of Congress Cataloging-in-Publication Data
Rylant, Cynthia.
Mr. Putter & Tabby run the race/Cynthia Rylant;
illustrated by Arthur Howard.
p.   cm.
Summary: Mr. Putter is convinced to run in a senior marathon with his
neighbor, Mrs. Teaberry, when he learns that second prize is a train set.
[1. Old age—Fiction.   2. Neighbors—Fiction.   3. Cats—Fiction.
4. Running races—Fiction.   5. Physical fitness—Fiction.]
I. Howard, Arthur, ill.   II. Title.   III. Title: Mr. Putter and Tabby
run the race.   IV. Title: Mister Putter & Tabby run the race.
PZ7.R982Mt   2008
[E]—dc22      2007003031
ISBN 978-0-15-206069-5

Printed in Singapore

First edition

A C E G H F D B

# 1

# Find Your Sneakers

It was April.

Mr. Putter and his fine cat, Tabby,

were full of April energy.

They always got extra energy in April.

Flowers were blooming,

birds were singing,

showers were showering. April!

Mr. Putter and Tabby felt it.

Mrs. Teaberry next door must have felt it, too.
She called Mr. Putter one April morning.
"There's a race," she said.
"A race?" asked Mr. Putter.
"A marathon!" said Mrs. Teaberry.

*Uh-oh*, thought Mr. Putter.

He was sure Mrs. Teaberry was going to ask him
to run the race with her.

"Will you run the race with me?"
asked Mrs. Teaberry.

Mr. Putter gave Tabby more cream.

"Aren't we too old to run a race?"
asked Mr. Putter.

"It's a *senior* marathon," said Mrs. Teaberry.
"Nothing but old people!"
Mr. Putter gave Tabby another biscuit.
"I have not run anywhere in thirty years,"
said Mr. Putter.
"I don't think I remember
how to run."

"There are prizes," said Mrs. Teaberry.

"Prizes?" asked Mr. Putter.

Mr. Putter *loved* prizes.

"One is a train set," said Mrs. Teaberry.

"Really?" asked Mr. Putter.

"With lights and switches and tunnels," said Mrs. Teaberry.

"Really?" asked Mr. Putter again.

"The train set is second prize,"
Mrs. Teaberry said.
Mr. Putter could not imagine a
train set being *second* prize.
It should be first.
"What is first prize?" asked Mr. Putter.
"Golf clubs," said Mrs. Teaberry.

Mr. Putter did not play golf.

He had tried once, but he and Tabby

kept getting lost.

Mr. Putter did not want golf clubs.

"I want that train set," said Mr. Putter.

"I knew you would," said Mrs. Teaberry.

"Find your sneakers."

# 2

# Toes and Tea

Mr. Putter started training for the marathon.

It was not easy.

It took him four days just to find his sneakers.

Then he had to work out.

Mr. Putter did not want to work out.

He wanted to eat muffins with Tabby.

But he knew that Mrs. Teaberry
was working out because
sometimes her good dog, Zeke,
ran by with a jump rope in his mouth.
(When Zeke wanted to play,
he took things and *ran*.)
So Mr. Putter had to work out, too.

He decided he would touch his toes
thirty times every day to make up for
the thirty years he'd forgotten to run.
The first time Mr. Putter tried to touch his toes,
he could not reach them.
He touched his knees
instead.

He touched his knees twice, and then he had
a cup of tea with Tabby.
The next time Mr. Putter tried to touch his toes,
he tried ten times, and he never got there.
But he enjoyed his tea with Tabby very much,
and he decided knees were just fine.

Zeke kept running by with his jump rope,
Mr. Putter kept touching his knees,
and Tabby had lots of tea.

Things were going great.

# 3

# Seniors!

It was finally the day of the senior marathon.
Mrs. Teaberry and Zeke were very excited.
Mrs. Teaberry had made special outfits for
both of them.
Zeke still had a jump rope in his mouth.
(Zeke had become very attached to his
jump rope.)

They all drove to the race.

When they arrived,

they saw many seniors lining up to run.

Zeke and Tabby got settled on top of the car.

Mr. Putter and Mrs. Teaberry got settled near
the starting line.

"I didn't know there were this many old
people," said Mr. Putter.

"Oh, we're everywhere!" said Mrs. Teaberry.

Mr. Putter looked around.

He saw a lot of old people touching their toes.

*Uh-oh,* thought Mr. Putter.

Everyone got in line.

"I hope you win that train set,"
said Mrs. Teaberry.

"I hope you come in first," said Mr. Putter.

The horn sounded.
And the seniors started running!

# 4

# The Race

Everybody passed Mr. Putter.
Everybody except two people.
Two people who tripped and fell and
never got up.
But everybody *else* passed Mr. Putter.

Mrs. Teaberry was way out in front.

Mr. Putter was way behind.

Tabby was asleep.
And Zeke had a jump rope in his
mouth and wanted to play.
That's when the race took a turn.

Suddenly there was confusion.

A dog with a jump rope was running the race!

All of the seniors tried to pass him.

They started bumping into one another.

Some of them got bumped right off the road.

Some of them stopped running
and started arguing.

More of them tripped.

But one of them wanted a train set so badly
that he ran right past everybody,
and grabbed hold of that jump rope,
and held on for dear life.
Zeke finally had someone to play with!
Zeke was so happy he ran even faster.
This made *Mr. Putter* run even faster.

Mr. Putter did not let go.

He wanted that train set.

He passed one runner after another

after another after another.

Then he passed Mrs. Teaberry.

And then . . .

HE WON THE RACE!!!

Everyone cheered! Everyone clapped!
Everyone was happy!

Everyone, that is, except Mr. Putter.

He had just won a set of golf clubs that had
no lights and no switches and no tunnels.
*Phooey!* thought Mr. Putter.

# 5

# Perfect Prizes

But things worked out after all.

Because who came in second? Mrs. Teaberry!

So she and Mr. Putter swapped prizes.

Mrs. Teaberry took her golf clubs home.

And Mr. Putter took home the best train set
he had ever seen in his life.

And for the rest of April, Mrs. Teaberry
and Zeke came back from the golf course
and went straight to Mr. Putter's house
to watch his trains.

Mr. Putter had a train hat.

Mrs. Teaberry had a golf hat.

Zeke had a jump rope.

Tabby had a nap.

And things worked out perfectly.

The illustrations in this book were done in pencil,
watercolor, and gouache on 250-gram cotton rag paper.
The display type was set in Artcraft.
The text type was set in Berkeley Old Style Book.
Color separations by SC Graphic Technology Pte Ltd, Singapore
Printed and bound by Tien Wah Press, Singapore
Production supervision by Christine Witnik
Designed by Arthur Howard and Brad Barrett

HALF HOLLOW HILLS COMMUNITY LIBRARY

3 1974 00929 4983

8/08(0)